ʔbédayine

its spirit

ʔbédayine
© 2019 Kaitlyn Purcell

Published by Metatron Press
1314 Ave. Lajoie
Montreal, Quebec
H2V 1P5

www.metatron.press

All rights reserved

Second Edition, First Printing

Editor | A. Light Zachary
Original cover art | Lorrie Dawn Purcell
Author photo | Brad Casey

Library and Archives Canada Cataloguing in Publication

Title: ʻbédayine / Kaitlyn Purcell.
Other titles: ʔbédayine
Names: Purcell, Kaitlyn, 1991- author.
Description: In title, ayn appears as international phonetic alphabet character for glottal stop.
Identifiers: Canadiana 20190163240 | ISBN 9781988355184 (softcover)
Classification: LCC PS8631.U734 B43 2019 | DDC C813/.6—dc23

We acknowledge the support of the Canada Council for the Arts, which last year
invested $153 million to bring the arts to Canadians throughout the country.

ʔbédayine
KAITLYN PURCELL

Metatron Press

ʔbédayine

FORT SMITH 9
FAREWELL 10
EDMONTON 18
HOME SWEET 19
BUS STOP NUMBERS 22
FALLING 24
WANDERROTTEN 25
ALARMKLOK 29
HEALTHY NUMBERS 34
ONE YEAR WITH STEVE 41
LOVE IS 44
2C-I TIMES THREE 47
SISTERS 53
TAMPONS 56
WATERFALL 57
PSCILOCYBINDAZE 60
PSILOCYBINZOO 71
MISPLACED ENDS 75
ECSTASY GHOSTS 76
SALVIA 83
PUSH AND BLOW 84
HIGHWAY OF TEARS 88
HANDEAD 94

For my sister, Lorrie.

FORT SMITH

sits just above the border between alberta and the northwest territories   dene metis dogrib and the fur trade washed up on the slave river and some of the caribou eaters were sent here in the 60s canadian government whispered a strange lullaby wanted their people all in one place and out of alberta   burned down their homes so they couldn't turn back a lullaby drowning in fiction instead of living off the land they were living in a town with no running water and no paint on their houses and children pushed into residential schools poisoned families and generations of family buried in alberta while the rest of them were laid to rest in the northwest   sundays spent with the creator and the church can still hear the whispering and whistles down in the crypt now the town is torn and whole   and smells like buffalo hide

FAREWELL

I spit chunks of vomit out into the grass. Always hated goodbyes, the way they twist my stomach and need to be erased with a six-pack of tall cans. Smoke from Thana's cigarette dances with horseflies while her long black hair sways in the sun. Our green van is parked next to a little outhouse, and the dirt roads stretch out north and south from us. We are only four hours from home, but we still have maybe ten to go.

Thana passes me the water bottle from her backpack and asks, "Did I ever tell you the story about the first time I drank?"

"Was that when you gave yourself a fat lip?"

"No—I was probably eleven and I stole a strawberry cooler from my sister's room. Thought it tasted pretty good, so it went down quick. My mom found me covered in red puke in the washroom. And you know what she did?"

"What?"

"She laughed. Then she threw a towel on me, shut the door. I cried for a while before my sister came in and helped me wash the puke off. Never asked my mom for help after that. And you know what? We need to look out for each other, you and me. And always make sure to wash the puke off when it gets tough. Y'know?"

"I promise to wash the puke out of your hair, but you gotta promise you won't leave me for some cute guy again," I laugh, before gargling some water and spitting it out.

"We'll see who's talking once you have a guy crawling all over you, too."

Thana puts out her cigarette and jumps back in the driver's seat. As the car pulls back onto the highway, I pull out my notebook and write.

loss turns to vomit   *can love bury these knots?*

in love and lost the way.   *goodbye, family.*

Never meant to wander, but I always did. Dad told me I was a runaway kid from the moment I began to walk on two feet. I guess when I was a toddler I was playing in my parents' closet and they thought I'd walked out into the forest or'd been taken by a black bear. Never was a good time, two overreactive parents and a runaway kid like me.

My dreams have also captured me, causing me to wander into other worlds. Always did like my sleep. I remember lots of my dreams, even ones from when I was still in the cradle. There's this one dream-inside-a-dream I've had since I was little. I first had it when I was just learning how to ride a bike—I remember, because I had another weird dream around that time where I lost control of the handlebars. But, this one dream-in-a-dream I keep having, it usually goes like this:

I wake up to the sounds of dogs barking and screeching. I go to the window, but it's still dark out. I walk down the hallway to try and find our dog, Bebi, but the front door is open. The screeching gets louder, so I run outside. As I step out the screeching goes silent. I become surrounded in light. A wind grabs me. It feels like I'm falling through heavy air.

That's when I actually wake up. This dream comes back every once in a while. It changes a little bit each time, but I always end up stuck in that blinding light. I always write down my dreams, and it's easier when they're bizarre. Sometimes they're so beautiful that it's hard to get out of bed. I live for the dreams about swimming in the ocean with the blue whales, orcas, hammerheads, and bottlenose dolphins.

Gravel turns to asphalt as Thana changes the CD with one hand on the wheel. She asks me to tell her a story.

"Hmm."

As the sounds of emo boys singing about broken hearts fill the car, I look out at the burnt-down landscape. Blackened skeletons of trees cast shadows over a ground green with new growth. I say, "Well, you know how my dad made me go to Sunday school, right? He thought it would be good for me, after Mom left. I would have to wear these dresses and these shiny black shoes. We would have to sit in the basement and read from the bible, and they would give us weird things to do, like colouring books of religious pictures. Well—this one week after Bebi died, I was really sad and I went to the washroom during Sunday school because I needed to cry. And while I was in there, I heard someone whistling outside the stall. But I looked, and there was no one there. I went back out and everyone was sitting silently, just working on their colouring. Creeped me out and I didn't know what to do, so I just went back to my seat."

"Did you tell your dad?"

"Yeah, he was upset. I didn't have to go back to Sunday school after that."

"Weird."

Thana's always loved my stories. I was pretty much a loner when we met, since I had a hard time speaking and most of the other kids thought it was weird.

We met in the tenth grade, around lunchtime. Instead of walking home, I walked towards my favourite place in the trees. That week, I had been hanging out with my cousin Johnny and I told him about the nightmares I was having, so he gave me some of his mom's painkillers to help me sleep. I took two, and I guess I ended up sleepwalking, or something, and my dad found me lying on the couch, drooling. A few days later, he found out that Johnny was stealing morphine from his mom, and asked if I had taken anything from him. I think I'm pretty good at making stories, but I'm also pretty terrible at lying. He yelled at me and told me not to turn out like my mom did. I spent that week afraid to say anything. I didn't want to be my mom. I couldn't even figure out how to be good enough to be anyone's friend.

That's when I met Thana. I was crying in the trees, throwing rocks at the branches, when I heard someone yell, "FUCK!" And saw her standing with a cigarette not too far from me. I held my breath, but it was too late. Her eyes found mine, and she started walking towards me. We became two strange, sad girls, sitting in the forest talking shit about the town and our families. After that, I was glad our families were messed up enough for us to become friends.

If not, we might have never left.

Pulling into the first big town in Alberta, we're greeted by flashing hotel signs and colourful fast food restaurants. It's probably the closest thing to Vegas that we'll ever get to see. We find a gas station, where I load up on Sour Patch Kids and Cool Ranch Doritos while Thana fills the car.

A thin guy walks into the store. The dusty blonde colour of his hair reminds me of Dylan, from back in Smith. Dylan, the boy who had strawberry coolers and a copy of *Night at the Roxbury* on VHS. The boy who ruined high school.

In the tenth grade, Thana was all googly-eyes over this boy at the ice cream store, and he invited us both over. I remembered feeling weird about going, but I knew it meant a lot to Thana by how she smiled on the way to Dylan's house. In his basement, the white of the hallways was painted over in layers of grease streaks left by fingers. They turned on the TV and Dylan put on *Night at the Roxbury*. He cracked open coolers for each of us before he fell into the plaid fabric of the couch. Thana joined him, while I sat to the side in the recliner.

My hands were tight around the curves of the bottle while I strained to keep my eyes on the TV. The plaid couch seemed to move beside me, but I was too scared to look. Thana and Dylan's breathing seemed to get louder while my insides were shaking.

> *stars in thana's eyes create constellations*
>
> *and the astrologers in her ears explain why*
>
> *pluto has fallen into her heart and her*
>
> *hands make their way to his*
>
> *thigh his dick shivers while wind*
>
> *mourns past the windows*

I put my cooler on the table and stood up. "You know, guys, I have to—I should go."

Thana stood up and grabbed my hand. "Just come sit with us. Relax."

She pulled me beside her, down on to the couch with Dylan, and my hands started to sweat.

"I always thought you two were beautiful," Dylan said. I kept my eyes glued on Will Ferrell and Chris Kattan, bobbing their heads and dancing in shiny suits. I gripped the edges of my shirt. Thana put her hands over my face. The shiny suits blurred into the dark and into the strawberry coolers. She pulled my gaze into hers, and then my lips onto hers.

After that day, it felt like everyone knew what we had done. They probably did. I spent more time avoiding people, spent more time in the trees.

I wave the junk food in the air before I jump back in the car. Thana laughs as I fasten my seatbelt. I pull out my astrology book and say, "So, your Venus is in Libra and my Venus is in Aries." Thana asks me what that means as we turn back on the highway.

EDMONTON

a city that sits on the north saskatchewan with histories of fort makers and papaschase garden thieves and land stolen so that people today can sit in their million-dollar homes while they look out their windows and say to themselves, "isn't this pretty?"   there are some parts of the city that they prefer to look away from   they look away from the migrating swarms of worn out looking folks east of city centre the black bags and shopping carts that swim upstream towards the bottle depot each day by the 6 o'clock closing   they look away at night when they walk beneath the white breast in the sky and they look away while teens wander alleys selling mom's medication cabinet   look away while a crying teenager runs out of an apartment building with only a towel wrapped around her look away when a guy dressed in all black walks towards the bridge   look away when the teenagers sneak out into the night   with their black jean jackets and glowing green hair

HOME SWEET

I'm already used to the taste of shit beer. I sit at the bar with a glass of the cheapest draft, waiting for Thana to finish her shift. It's been a month since we got here and I still don't know how to shake the feeling of pointed looks and quiet lips everywhere I go. Everyone here, too, confuses my silence with weakness.

Nothing feels right.

What is this? Am I lost in my own skin? I feel like the more of a freak I become, the more I want to embody the parts of me that the world seems to hate.

Sad girl.

I'm just a child again, caged at night in my cradle. The moon pours through the trees outside my window, and the shapes of my mobile twist against the wall. Am I crying because the shadows scare me, or because all I want to do is dance with the darkness?

I finish my drink. The bartender, Dave, asks if I need another. Thana is off serving one of the tables full of big white men with their bloated hands and bellies.

I say, "Please," but Dave has already poured one for me.

There is so much noise in the city, so much fluorescence and weird stank everywhere.

I miss the trees. Here it's all cement.

The apartment is close enough to the bar and other stuff that we can find our way everywhere on foot, or one quick bus ride. We each pay $281 a month to share a room big enough for a bed and our garbage bags of clothes. No TV, no internet, no phone, no need for extra costs or extra takers-up of space. My only excesses are my sketchbooks, pencils, and three books my sister gave me. The astrology book; a book on dream interpretations, since she always said I have the weirdest dreams; and another called *Go Ask Alice*, which she said was better than any book I'd ever be taught in school.

My glass is empty, again. I just want to go home, but Thana likes it when I'm here to walk her home. She says Dave creeps her out.

My glass is full, again.

Maybe I just need to become a full-time astrologer. Or a tarot-reader. I hate retail.

Thana's so lucky—she just gets to help people drink.

I help people find the changing room. I help them pay for their cheap sweatshop clothes. I help them find their size. I help them decide which dress will turn on their boyfriend.

My glass is empty.

"Ready to go?"

We wander back towards the apartment. My legs are still heavy from standing all day. Thana puts her arm around me.

"How much did you drink?"

"Not enough."

"Don't you work tomorrow?"

"Don't worry about it."

Thana laughs and I join in as the streets fade around us, the storefronts and the bus shelters.

"Can I ask you something?"

She nods, holding on to my shoulder.

"Can you wash my hair for me sometime? And braids, too. I miss that."

"Sure, Ronnie."

BUS STOP NUMBERS

The bus is as exhausting as it is marvelous. The bus is a place that takes me to live in purgatory for five to eight hours a day.

The person sitting across from me on the bus is wearing a puffy brown coat and her hair is bright, caustic blonde. Yesterday she called her mother, who told her to fuck off. But maybe I'm just mistaking the bags under her eyes for sadness. I won't ever know, and maybe shouldn't care. Maybe I should be so full of myself that I float to the moon. Should I love her more than I love myself? Or is it that the more I love myself, the more I will become able to love the world? Can I fill myself with so much love that there's no longer room for anything else inside me? So full of love, will I really float away? Or will my love for the world sink roots in to keep me here?

Why am I so concerned?

I feel eyes on me.

Blinking my thoughts away, I notice a beautiful tanned man staring at me from the back of the bus.

He looks like a mixture of white and native. His eyes are lightness, and his body is gold. I look away for a minute before I feel like I can look back. He gets off the bus at the end of Jasper Avenue, but he glances back again before he leaves.

It smells like someone lit a joint in here. The smell wafts towards me as we wait to leave the Jasper Place bus terminal. The smell marries another: parfum alcoholic. I am on a bus of addicts and it's 8 PM on a Tuesday. I check my phone—it's at 4%, so I can't listen to music. I try to read some of my dream book, instead.

Dreaming about the end of the world signifies a big change in your life.

The lights are dim inside the bus, and the sun has already gone down. It looks like the bus is sitting in space, blackness everywhere except for the buzzing dim lights inside this rectangular box. Somewhere near the front, a child screams.

FALLING

On one of those rare days we both have off, Thana comes to me with some little pink pills of ecstasy that she got from her co-worker. I guess everyone here is all about ecstasy. Each pill is stamped with a little heart or bumblebee. "She said, these will make you fall in love with the world."

I don't know much about ecstasy. I don't even think anyone from back home ever did ecstasy, or anything like it.

Thana takes me to a party and we swallow our pills.

running is flying and love runs everywhere

it was waiting 17 years sings like broken

sunglasses, tape around the head dancing

jaw clenching dancing jaw clenching until

glow stick painted walls asphyxiate

    overtones of isolation

WANDERROTTEN

I wake up in an echo. I don't know what the fuck is going on. I don't know when I lost control, or how many days I've been on E. I'm coasting through the work week; autopilot pill-poppin' child. *I'm so high.* But today I wake up and the world is an echo. At work, it's all a blur behind a blur. I assume it's my drug habit, or how much I may have forgotten to eat. No need to tell me what I already know.

I remind myself that I don't care if I die. Better to die beautiful, right?

I leave work and I'm not sure where I am. Granite is made from the heart of my habit, infinite fractals of methylphenidate and amphetamines. I break bottles on the sidewalk.

Ecstasy, where were you?

Deja vu destiny.

Food becomes a distant memory. I begin to fall or black out at least once a day. I can't bend down, can't move too fast, fuck stairs (broke my toe the other day), and lying down makes it harder to get up. I'm walking and falling and falling and falling. My teeth are yellowing. The skin on my legs looks like old bananas.

A guy from work with a big rounded face and crinkled eyes says I need to stop. I need to put down the drugs. But I like to mash my brain. Mash it until it's mush enough to wash down with a bump of ketamine. I tell the guy to back off, because I've made friends with bad days, withdrawal symptoms, my body is doing strange things, it's floating in a fever. Floating in a nightmare, upside down, I can't find my body because my insides are the surface of the sun, it feels like toilet paper rubbing against my teeth, an itch that only hurts when I rub it, my veins are screaming, *you fucking cunt whore!*

I've been living in bed, or out meeting the baby-face dealer. Sweating beneath a blanket. Eating is out of the question—if only Thana could see me dumping out my dinner in the garbage. I like to pretend to be well fed and I walk around with sunglasses at night. I pretend it's my new thing. Pills are my new style. It is something that blends between the colours of my dreams and right into the blue powder on my eyelids. I'm twisting into red. I ask you the same question four times and forget what we were talking about. Short term memory loss, I hope. *This is all just an experiment.* Let's see what happens when I take all the pills.

Throw five in. Five more. Last time I took eight and barely got high at all.

The feeling floats over my body and I end up in Thana's car, heading to the legislature grounds with some of our new friends. Our fractured pupils and dilated jaws become the moon when it blocks out the sun, hailstorms, magic disguised as nightmares. Clammy synth pop disperses across my skin like bubbling fizz candies. I bounce around in the passenger seat, smoking cigarettes with the window down. When we reach the legislature grounds, the sun is rising.

Standing in a shallow pool, dark electric clouds sway into the pink of sunrise. They form a circle, leaving the piece of sky above me untouched.

A hole.

An awful beauty that haunts, that speaks to me.

The whole world sits in the sky and the world is ending. Pink clouds swirl into funnels. Twirling pink fingers try to reach the earth.

Back at Thana's friend's house, I run into the basement and turn on the news.

Tornados are sucking up cars in intersections, *people are dying*, the world is dying, and *the sky is falling*.

I wake up and it's 6:45. How did I sleep so long? *FUCK—I need to call work.*

I call my boss, but she sounds confused. My words fall into my phone like a game of 52-pickup, cards are flying all over and crashing into the ground. She tells me I'm not making any sense, that it's only 6:45 in the morning. I'm not even scheduled for work today. I guess I only slept for twenty minutes.

quasi-stars penetrate the "indian" that i was   sky evolves into an inviting shadow   allow light to enter the third eye, brightening holistic   phantom of her words   denesuline: "the real people"   i don't like thinking about the doubling of shadows as midnight approaches

    the light bares healing stories.

        moving out of slum indigo

ALARMKLOK

A week has passed since I saw the tornadoes, and I can't stop staring out the window, waiting for them to come back. The texture of the unfinished ceiling matches my brain, and the poor lighting matches the dilation of my eyes. I like the nakedness of my space, the bed with no sheets. This is my hole in the wall. The unclean dishes, the fruit flies, spiders, shadow spiders, and the fabric hanging over the window. I don't think I have a job anymore. Thana comes home less and less.

Took too many pills this month. Shredded thoughts. Don't care if I die here. Can barely stand, keep falling on the concrete floor. I lay for a while before trying to crawl back into bed.

I will get up later.

Dreams amalgamate with walls.

It's 59:75, and I am late. I run to the washroom to get ready. I run back to the bedroom and check the weather through the window. I lift the sheet and through the window I can see tornadoes everywhere, tearing apart the neighborhood. Houses have been turned into holes. I turn around and run. But it's too late. *Run*. The tornado is pulling me in. I am held by wind. There is silence as it roars until there is no more room in my ears. *Run down.* Air pulls me in. The tornado takes me.

I wake up.

Why is the world always fucking ending?

I turn over and the TV is on. An infomercial for Slap Chop says: "You're gonna love these nuts!"

It's only 3:14 AM. I must have been sleeping for a while. I try to get up, but my legs still don't work. I crawl to the fridge, pull out a juice box and some bread. I throw the bread down my throat, chase it with the concentrated orange drink.

There are beer bottles all over the counter. I count one, two, three, four, five, six, seven, eight, fuck. I lose count, but I know I didn't drink those. I use the fridge handle to pull myself up. Stars flood my eyes until everything is black. I wait it out, as usual, holding on to the countertop. After a minute, my vision comes back to me, and I can see that the bathroom light is on. It seems a mile away. I use the walls to pull myself closer.

When I reach the light of the bathroom, I find Thana curled next to the toilet. She is half-naked, her breasts exposed, and there are blood streaks on the door. She is partly singing and partly crying. It's the saddest thing I've ever heard, sadder than cries of mourning. I let myself drop next to her on the floor. I brush her hair out of her face. When I look into her eyes, mine begin to water. I hold her until I feel her breath slow. "Thana, I think I'm dying," I whisper. "I could hardly walk here from the bed."

She says, "You need to get off those pills."

I nod, taking in the reek of beer and vomit on her breath. I say, "And you need to quit this drinking."

She stands up. She offers a hand and pulls me up to stand with her, but when I stand the stars and blackness come again, and I tell her that I can't see anything.

She leads us back to bed and pulls the blankets up over our heads. I play with her knotted hair while she rubs my cheeks.

I drift into sleep, begin to dream: *The city is covered in the greenest grass and canola field-yellow houses. A tornado is tearing through it all. Homes spit out and twisted. Vibrant yellow deaths of childhood memories and soft beds. I run through the streets. The tornado pulls me in. I am torn into pieces and every piece is spinning in circles.*

The next day, Thana comes home from work with a bag of groceries and a gram of weed. "This will help us both sober up a bit," she says as she looks me over. "You're wasting away. You really need to eat."

She asks me if I've ever tried blades. She takes two butter knives and tucks them into the red coil of the stovetop. She rinses out an old Coke bottle, cuts off the bottom and says, "It's really intense, but I think we need to do it this way for it to work." Pulling out the heated knives, she balances a bit of weed on top of one and presses the other down over it while she places her Coke-bottle funnel over the smoke, sucks it all in. She holds in the smoke for a second before letting it drift out of her mouth, nice and slow. She prepares the blades for me, passing me the funnel. I inhale the hot smoke, try to hold it in. Fire lungs force me into a coughing fit. Every inch of my body feels like heavy liquid stones. I walk to the bed, and my eyes want to close.

"Thana, do you have any food?"

She laughs and opens a big bag of plain Lays, passing it over to me. I smile and eat. I give up on trying to keep my eyes open, but I can't stop smiling and eating.

I drift into sleep, begin to dream:

The world is turned inside out. Our solar system has rearranged itself. The earth sits in the orbit where Uranus was. We stole its moons. One moon chases the other as they drift across the sky. Cold air swallows us. Heavy snow. The sun is too far to feel it on our skin. A famine for wildflowers. The world is going to end.

Why is the world always fucking ending?

HEALTHY NUMBERS

I think I must have slept for a week straight. Thana seems to spend most days working and feeding me. She says she doesn't mind, and that what I have is harder to kick. I love her more than anything.

My nerves feel like short-circuiting wires. Electric flammable insides. Weed seems to be the only thing that makes the feeling go away.

I've started to develop an appetite for milk and canned pineapple. French fries, too.

i won't be anyone anymore

until i apologize for swearing

Days pass, and I'm finally feeling like I can walk outside again.

in front of the sudden dial tone

like rug burns on my knees,

I start looking for a new job. The movie theatre seems easy enough.

a book with all the stories

about his life.   *i cry*

Everyone seems to love the way my skin is stretched over my bones. (*Wow, Ronnie, you look amazing!*) Near death, I've become beautiful.

On the way home from a shift at the movie theatre, I see that same beautiful man from months ago, sitting way in the back of the bus.

Suddenly he is beside me, saying, "Hey."

I say, "Hi."

He passes me a little piece of paper and whispers, "Call me later?"

I nod as he gets up and off the bus.

The little piece of paper has his name and number on it.

Jake.

I wonder if I'm going to die tonight. I'm sitting in Jake's apartment on his leather couch. White walls, wooden coffee table. Clean, no clutter. Nothing like the mess at home. He pours expensive rum over a short glass of ice. "Need chase?" I smile, and he's already back and forth from the kitchen with a bottle of Dr. Pepper.

He tells me that he's surprised I texted him, and that I actually came over. It is hard to tell whether he's being honest, but I don't think I really care. The shape of his face and the warm tones of his skin and hair invite me into some part of myself that I want to see. I want to know where he is going to take me.

We exchange some parts of our past. I tell him about how I was recently addicted to ecstasy, but that I'm fine now. He tells me that he was part of some gangs before, used to get in fights, and he was diagnosed with psychosis.

"Psychosis?"

"Didn't feel anything for a while."

Will he strangle me to death to feel something? Or maybe he'll kidnap me—or, rather, keep me here. My face feels tense. He's probably twice my size, so there would be nothing I could do. I take another sip of my drink, and he asks how long I was an addict.

"Four months, maybe. Weed and sleep helped me kick it."

"That's good, that you managed to get out of it."

He takes his hand to my hair, lightly threads it in between his fingers. I look up at him as his face begins to approach mine. My tongue slides into his mouth.

He pulls away and says, "Less tongue."

I let his mouth lead mine into achy legs, vibrating goosebumps from inside my ovaries to my inner thighs, like magenta melted over laguna blue. He is so beautiful, with his slutty arrangement of thick hairy trunks and twisting roots around my smooth birch branches. Arms through arms. The art of his shoulders sings into me like bees feeding on lilacs. I've been stung so many times before. I wonder if he will ever love me the way I smell the lilacs. Or that smell before rain. I can smell it now and I cry joy and dig my nails into his back. The air moves so quickly between us.

I always knew I was a tornado in a past life.

It's been three weeks since we first fucked. In the downtown Tim Hortons bathroom, we stand in blue light. A guy enters, and I giggle. He grins at me and Jake and goes into a stall, while we continue to crush pills into toilet paper. This must be the cure to everything.

Jake passes me blue dust wrapped in a cotton pillow. His pretty face tells me that this will save me. I can't help but think and feel that this is true love, me and him. Two weirdos drawn together like metal and magnets. Eyes shatter eyes, and my body melts in ecstasy before the drug can even hit me. We leave with our stomachs turning, arm in arm. We take the next bus to the Mill Creek ravine.

It is warm out and we stumble underneath the bridge. "I think we were meant to be, right here, you know," he says to me as I smile and say, "This is perfect. The air. The sky. And you are so beautiful. And I feel so beautiful. This is it." I laugh with all my teeth (YES!) and he pulls me in, his arm around my shoulders. I am in love, each cell of my body is glistening with joy, the air of all that is alive wraps around us. Every tree and star brushes us with light.

he falls in love for an hour and i fall in love for a month   blue dust-filled holes and invertebrate wishes at midnight   falling from the moon and into the earth's atmosphere my body is on fire   pick me up again and name me 3 AM

We walk and walk until we find a patch of grass that sings the song of our high. We fall into it and into each other and laugh in our chaotic embrace.

These drugs fill the potholes on the worn-out roads that exist inside me. Every heartbreak, every terrible thing, everything that ever begged me to cry is erased.

I walk into the lagoon of my dreams.

My phone rings, and I laugh. It's Thana. She asks me where I am. "I'm somewhere in the trees—the grass? This guy—Jake—where are you?" I snort before she tells me to meet her at some address. I repeat it to Jake, and he knows where it is. Nearby. We roll over and up and shuttle into the streets again.

I fall into another dream: *I'm driving through the night, the sky lit with shooting stars all bursting down towards me. The world is ending and I'm too far to reach my family.*

When I wake up, I'm curled into Jake's body. Thana brings me a glass of water. I shut my eyes and smile as I gulp until the glass is empty. I listen to the sounds of Thana struggling to ignite her lighter, the way she breathes as she ingests the smoke. The smell of weed unearths me.

ONE YEAR WITH STEVE

I walk around a barred-window building, its skin like undercooked fries, with Thana and her boyfriend until we spot an underwhelming sign that says, "The Studio".

The party is full of men with baggy hoodies. A group of rappers line the stage, filling the venue with their words and heavy beats. I feel silly standing here, so we find a spot in a room with couches and strange beams everywhere. We find a little glass room and stand inside of it, drinking our bottle of spiced rum and coke. We giggle at how out of place we are and how alien this place is from regulations and rules. Underage drinking, and no one gives a fuck.

I look up and, through the glass wall, meet the gaze of a guy with dark hair and eyes, sitting on the couch across the room. I look back at Thana and giggle.

"Ronnie, I think that guy's staring at you."

He is.

He motions for me to join him. I look back to Thana, and she ushers me away.

His eyes say a hundred things. There is a past that lives there, and in the large scabs on his cheeks. He tells me his stories about how he's from Toronto, a product of rape left to be adopted by a Somali family, by brothers that taught him the neighbourhood. He used to be a little white boy with a broken heart, but they taught him right. They showed him the way to beat respect into the streets. The people that were there, he showed them how to be scared. The alcohol in my blood allows me to rest my head in his lap and I stare up into his face. He is so strange and amazing.

> *smell of vodka and hennessy*
>
> *drawn together like two pisces*
>
> *with open hearts and crowns*
>
> *of dandelions love at first love*
>
> *is first painted in the way*
>
> *the summer winds toss me aside*

He walks me home and tucks me into bed.

can we ever see the ocean

the way you hold my smile?

When I wake up, he is gone. But I'm still searching for his eyes, the ones that spoke about the love he never got as a kid.

LOVE IS

As we make a left turn through a busy intersection, the right door in the back flips open. I clench my seat, holding my breath. The door slams shut as the car straightens out, and I panic my arms to lock it.

The driver looks back for a second, "Ah, shit. Yeah, that door doesn't lock up too good."

We drive into the anus of the city, by the government buildings across from Chinatown. I get out and light a cigarette. Copper glass reflects the residue of the sun, and the day dips into the edges of the sky.

A young man walks up to me. I smile when I see him. He has a big dick in his pants and little bags of drugs in his pockets. He likes to buy me French fries and hot chocolate. He likes to open all the doors.

We wander, and he trades little bags for $10 bills until it's pretty late, and we're standing in the yellow-white fluorescent light of an underground parkade. A girl is crouched down with a glass pipe filled with white smoke that's thick like coffee cream. She guzzles the high and moves her body in a scattered rippling rhythm as she exhales. "Jib-tech," she calls herself. A golden heart fucked up with the crack fashion—a tight tank top and cargo pants. She likes to wiggle her butt when she walks, sing to the sky as she moves across the downtown sidewalk.

I meet a man who says, "I'd spend $2000 for a night with you." Flattery darts over me before I begin to feel like a piece of furniture. I am the couch lost in the woods, and I don't have the mouth to say, "Fuck off."

We burn the broken furniture. Pale wooden ghosts prod my knees. City park picnics with cigarettes and crack pipes, the Wiggling Body sells mom's Ativan and says, "Show me the way to the cigarette garden." Large hand on my back gently nudges. Show me the way. A kite slowly falls into a tree.

Under the influence of the pet rabbit that fell stiff in my hands at the age of six, of these hands that held lifeless long ears and soft brown fur. The influence of melancholy and insanity. I both regret and enjoy. I apologize with absence and elusion.

It feels better falling down.

Only pretty girls wither away. These boys love to see my bones, and they love the legs-open lullaby. I sing better when I'm high.

I like to see the moth written across his eyes. *I am your moonlight, baby.*

Slutty, sketchy, skanky, scum—the S sounds kiss

the space between my teeth. We're going to die anyways, might as well die in the hole of the high. Here, the whole world holds me. The jib-techs meet in the city gardens. It's safer being forest fairies, setting up tents in the river valley, filling the tent with that wicked wet-dog smell, the fog of meth.

"I love you," he says. My hollow cheeks blush. The dealer that needs me. I need his drugs and to look into his pretty brown eyes. I keep wanting to get hit with feelings, to be deformed with ecstasy.

I like it when your heart seeps into your eyes; I like to see it bleed.

2C-1 TIMES THREE

I.

"Should we?"
"May as well."

Placing one of the tiny blue pills in my hand, Steve drops one on top of his blue tongue stained from the free popsicles he received earlier from a guy with a broken freezer. He takes out a bottle of Diet Pepsi to swallow his pill, hands the bottle over and I swallow mine.

"Let's find someplace to sit, and I'll try to sell some of these."

My eyes wander as the crowd of toothy asymmetrical smiles and scents of unwashed clothes approaches. Laughs are exchanged, transactions are made. I am swallowed slowly by the cement, until a girl with black stringy hair walks by with her hips out and sings:

"You know, it's hard out here for a pimp!"

In the center of downtown, the lights grow brighter under the darkening sky, a parking sign flickers OPEN in neon green, thrusts against my eyes, digs deep into my brain. Lights that turn on and off inside the tall buildings strobe and swim through the summer air,

lightening, darkening, pressing inside my frail skull—
Fuck this. Shit's getting too real.
I start off down the sidewalk. Steve is laughing with a group of jib-techs and street kids. I find myself on a bus for two seconds before I'm back home. In my room, I flick the light switch on, and the kaleidoscope attacks me from all sides, tracers for tracers, sky-blue walls are fucking the brains out of the lemon-yellow hanging sheets, and the rainbow enters my body, tearing me apart.

II.

"YES?"
"YES!"

Tiny blue pills jump from our hands onto tongues stained blue from the red, white, and blue rocket pops, followed by a stream of Diet Pepsi, black aspartame thrusts into the pits of our stomachs where strong acids suck on the pill until the chemicals soak into our blood, chemicals fornicate with our minds, bodies, third eyes, giving birth to bastard grins. "OKAY, GO!"

A crowd forms a rainbow around us, pill-poppers, toothy asymmetries, musk and shit stain stinks, greasy hairs. Pills are sold for $5 bills as it begins to rain for a brief millisecond, laughing, fist pumps, fisting the air, fisting with laughter, and "You know it's hard out here for a pimp!" fisting our ear canals.

Our pill-popping minds are totally wanked, the surrounding skyscrapers become glowing phallic statues, their glow flickers so hard that it pummels our pill-poppin' eyes, threatening the collapse of downtown. A nearby parkade sign screams at the top of its neon lungs, "I am open! ENTER ME! OPEN! I AM WIDE FUCKING OPEN!"

Increased heart rate, dilated pupils, toothy asymmetries, lip licking (*will the real pervert please stand up?*), mismatched bedroom eyes, the musk of the rainbow, the pill-popper's back tenses, arms crossed, "FUCK THIS SHIT, LET'S GO!"

Across cold cement, light punishes the peripheries, walking, floating, running, stepping on the bus, the bus departs, "Don't fucking do it—don't look out the window."

III.

FUCK YEAH

downtown's latest perversion:
a chemical amalgam of psychedelics form the tipsy
brush strokes of starry night across empty cement
blue pills for blue tongues the unduly fluorescence
musk rainbow stank a tooth hard pimp
and the sky freckled with light is penetrated
by the tips of the westin and telus while pill-poppin' animals
muster by a bronze statue called   "TRADERS"
and fucking fractals of jizz fly into eyes filled with sand
an empty pussy and loaded cock rifle through
memories   3AM   they received our messages
dialect of the world of sheetless mattresses
and a plethora of trojan & durex
walking through the inside of a kaleidoscope

i'm so high

SISTERS

Joey screams, "We have to leave right-fucking-*now*!"

He's such a sweet guy. It's scary to see him so urgent, frightened. Everyone is flying out of the basement while an array of misery pours in. I'm still looking for my sweater. My eyes are all over the ground, searching, but I'm soon surrounded by a flood of people whose darkness is so deep that it blinds me. I follow a blurry path out of the tunnel as their silence fills the room. I break for the hallway near the stairs, but two girls jump out in front of me. They break the thread of light.

"What are you lookin' at us for?"

Their faces are harder than anything I've ever seen before. One of them has lightened her long hair to caramel, while the other is wearing a hat and baggy boy's clothes. Both native. I don't understand. Why do they want to hurt a cousin, a sister?

My mouth is too frightened to find the words, so I push past them.

Caramel-Hair jumps on top of me. Her fists, vicious, pounding both sides of my head.

My body collapses into the fetal position.

Too weak to fight back.

One-two. One-two.

Her fists, my face, my head, the floor.

One-two. One-two.

All I can see is my hair tangled in the light.

One-two. One-two.

The world spins as she keeps punching until someone pulls her off. Arms carry me outside, but every voice I hear is muffled.

My left eye is swollen shut. I can't stop crying.

What kind of pain did these girls have to live through to hurt another native girl like this? We were supposed to be sisters.

We are supposed to be sisters.

tornado took a water bottle from her backpack

    our solar system has rearranged itself

        into a six-pack of tall cans

    smoke stole the moons

      i remember feeling weird

        about the "indian" that i was

TAMPONS

You never know what might happen. Sometimes I wonder if my heart could burst or if my brain could implode. Sometimes I wonder if all the trees can hear us. Sometimes I can't tell what my thoughts are.

> *my dreams have been the only thing*
> *that make them go away*

I walk with Thana to the parking lot where the dealer said he would meet us. As we pass the Esso, I notice a young guy running out, hunched over with his arms around something in his coat.

"Don't you know that guy?"

Thana looks up as a clerk runs out of the Esso, waving his arms in the air.

The clerk yells, "Hey! Come back here!"

The guy nearly runs past us but stops.

He says, "Thana! Shit, I had to steal these for my girlfriend!" He opens up his coat and reveals a box of tampons.

We laugh, and the guy turns back to the clerk and yells, "Sorry, I need these for my girlfriend! She's bleeding, man!" He looks back at us and grins as he runs off down the sidewalk.

WATERFALL

It's my first real Valentine's Day date, and it feels like my heart is full of the warmest conversations about world peace and love for all things. Steve holds my hand as we make our way to the mall for dinner and a movie. I'm wearing my favorite boots and blue pleather coat. His black hair is spiked with gel, and he's wearing his favorite zip-up with the pattern that reminds me of the forest if the forest were turned into ice cream.

>*i live for dreams about oceans*
>
>>*decorated with broken sidewalk*
>
>*he shows them how to be a cigarette*
>
>>*dancing with a horsefly*

As we wait for the crosswalk by the mall, our eyes are drawn right, to where a group of maybe twenty kids swarm between a house and the chain-link fence. Smaller kids surround the taller kids. They seem to sway together in violent bursts and waves.

"I think they're beating someone up," I whisper. "We need to do something."

Steve pulls me closer, speaks in a low-hard voice. "There's too many of them. Just—come on, let's go."

The light turns green and he leads me across the road and away. I keep my head turned, my eyes on the space near the fence as we reach the other side of the street.

The swarm disperses. The kids start to run out in all directions. Some of the older ones run with their long legs past me and Steve. One tall native guy with short hair runs by. His eyes lock with mine as he runs past us, and they are filled with a hollow left by anger. He looks like he could have been a very beautiful person.

Then—I pull hard on Steve's hand to get him to turn around, lift my other hand, point across the street as our friend Joey staggers out from behind the fence, looks our way with his arms around his chest.

We run towards him. His skin looks like it has been turned into chalk, and the edges of his face are sinking downwards. We put our arms around him, carry him towards the light of the bus terminal.

I scream, "Call an ambulance!"

All the people waiting for their buses swarm around us. Multiple voices speak into their phones at once.

An ambulance to the West Edmonton Mall bus terminal. A young man, he looks really pale. I think he's bleeding.

Joey says in a weak voice, "I think they stabbed me," as he unzips his puffy coat. From inside the coat, a pool of blood falls and hits the cement floor with a splash. I feel my heart sink into the spinning space around me.

Steve pulls me back and away. "You shouldn't see this."

I stumble outside, trying to breathe between each sob. Two bus drivers come up to me, and one passes me a bottle of water while the other gently hugs my shoulder with his hand.

Breathe.

Standing at the bus terminal late at night with my first love. I'm anywhere but here, I am drifting underwater, the sounds above the surface are muffled.

Why am I drifting so far?

Why did I love him so much?

I look up to the bus beside me, see the could-be-beautiful native guy watching from the very back seat. I point my finger up towards him. Tell the drivers, "That's one of them. The ones who did it."

awful beauty that makes it hard to get out of bed

PSCILOCYBINDAZE

"Trust me—I'll only get high if I eat a half ounce." Kris devours his bag of shrooms while Steve and I trade wide-eyed glances. We start on our smaller portions of wrinkly golden caps, dirty eggshell stems. Last time we got high, we laughed at my failed attempts to pull on my saggy black boots, so we fell over in the hallway, rolled around until our stomachs ached and I pissed a little. This time, we sit with our jackets and shoes already on as we gnaw on the woodchip texture that tastes like a bag of unsalted Spitz. We head outside, where the sky is a blue that sits in the garden at night whispering sexual innuendos. We find and follow the narrow wooden path to the river and over the bridge.

Kris is frolicking as he walks. "This is going to be so fucking cool, guys, this night is a glorious one—feel the air, the fucking water, and those fucking trees. Look at it all, holy fuck."

the kind of blue that sits   whispering sew stank sipping and slipping, buried beneath midnight's latest perversion, lost stomachs ached, nearly pissed their pants, gnawing on sheets, a sheet of plastic protects the mattress from unsalted spitz, trust me i'll only get high if i eat its arms,   the whispers, the echo of the golden caps and dirty eggshell stems

We sit on a cool, thick blanket of grass. To the west, the cliff overlooks the river, out towards the city core. Quasi-stars penetrate the shadows as midnight approaches. The lights get brighter, the sky evolves into an inviting shade of indigo (*on psilocybin mushrooms, pupils dilate allowing light to enter, brightening, opening the third eye*). The grass comes alive with a darker green that breathes on my ankles. Kris's eyes are wide; he begins to roll towards me, rolling nearly on top of my legs while looking into Steve's face with a burning intensity.

"I just want to fight, you know—I JUST WANT TO FUCKING FIGHT!"

"Man, we just have to chill, you know. Just take in the high."

"No, I need to fight!" He inhales hard and looks at me, "Do you wanna fight?"

Steve laughs, "Man, just cool off. She doesn't want to fight."

I look down at the grass and pick at the blades, but Kris rolls back on top of my legs. I jerk my body back and shuffle towards Steve. I can't hide how fear pulls at the sides of my cheeks. I pick the blades and the green is breathing. Steve puts his arms around me, says quietly, "Shit—I'm sorry about him." I nod slowly, still picking at the grass. Steve jumps to his feet and says, "Okay, let's start walking. Maybe someone will want to fight you over there." Kris leaps into the air, smiling with his arms out, "Really? I need to fight—where are they? I need to *fight!*" He walks up to Steve with his chest pushed out, rapid heavy breath, moist flecks of something flying from his mouth. Steve looks at me and shrugs. I keep my arms crossed, wanting to coil into myself until I disappear far away from Kris, who's spinning, jumping up and down. He runs across the field, down the street. Steve grabs my hand and pulls me the other way. We run. My eyebrows lift, my mouth hangs open (*OH!*), my chest pounds with joy. I can still hear Kris in the distance (*WANNA FIGHT?*), we run faster away from his voice, cement fluctuates beneath our feet, shifting, seething at the feeling. Our thin and unworn hands grip each other tightly, a soft reassuring touch. Giggling and skipping, I pull at Steve to stop and catch my breath. I laugh and jump into his arms. The smell of cigarette smoke and leather holds me close, the prickles of his face bury into my neck.

We keep walking until we find a big, beautiful tree. Looking down at the ground around Steve's shoes, I say, "I'm sorry I couldn't handle it—he was just getting way too close."

"Fuck, whatever. I barely know the guy. He's fucked for thinking he needs a half-O."

Steve releases his grip of my hands, but continues to hold his palm to mine, touching the tips of our fingers together. He looks down the road, squinting at the distant neon green-red-orange-red sign: *7-Eleven*.

"Should we grab some candy?"

The sign grows, illuminating our bodies and eliminating shadow. We turn into the store, stomachs fluttering (*this place is too busy*), and every eye in the space seems to touch our psilocybin-filled-bodies. We smile with our lips closed and dart through over the store. I spot the 5-cent candies, while Steve walks to the Slurpee station. I grab a small plastic bag and start to pick at the boxes with a tiny set of tongs. Jelly frogs, whales, eggs, strawberry marshmallows, sour soothers—

"Ronnie!"

I almost drop the bag as I turn to see a few of Thana's friends standing beside me, "Oh! How's it going?"

"Just stoned, grabbing munchies," Thana's friend says as the other one smiles through red eyes and shows off his white teeth.

"Nice. Yeah. I'm messed, too." Lowering my voice, I say, "We took shrooms." I can't contain an enormous grin that feels like ten fingers tickling the insides of my cheeks. I nearly fall into a fit of laughter when Steve walks up with his cup of blue slush. He nods at the red-eyed guys, and I wave goodbye as Steve leads me to the cash. I can barely hold in ten-fingered-tickling laughter as I hand the cashier my bag of candy and a $20 bill.

The cashier asks, "How many?"

Convulsions of warm blankets break through me, eyes watering, and I throw out a number (26!?). I'm barely able to pull myself back together.

passing out pisces, keep going until you are covered with scarlet and violet, shaking eyes, touching, touching amalgamated drug habits,

    who cowered in the unshaven sky,

        who cut their wrists with blades of grass;

            the air falls over

We find ourselves falling back onto a slight hill full of grass next to a few tall pines. Moonlight walks across the field and onto our bodies. I roll onto my side and place a jelly whale into my mouth. As I chew, my teeth struggle to break down the gelatin, my taste buds fail me (*um, this doesn't taste like anything*), I toss the bag aside, laughing until my stomach aches. Steve laughs (*yeah, this slurpee tastes like shit*). He rolls onto his side and looks at me, inhales, exhales (*love*). Our eyes and hands wander over one another while I drink in the sky and drifting clouds. Exhale (*love*). We get up, walk back in the direction of the comfort of a bed. Down towards the bridge, we see red and blue lights pulsating in the distance. We look at each other, stand up straight (*relax, keep calm*) as we get close enough to see what's going on. A cop car blocks the sidewalk ahead. As Steve grabs my hand and we cross the road (act normal), I look back to see a thin naked guy lying on the ground beside the car. The cop, a blonde woman, hands on her hips, bends over the guy as he calls out, "You're a troll!"

"Oh, fuck—that's Kris. Dude better not see us," Steve says to me as we start to shuffle back home.

kris devours the ceiling, the walls, they start to munch on their portions of wrinkly strangulation, a kite falls into a fit of laughter, warm towels and daisy chains, just take in the mustard yellow, dim sum for everyone, the north saskatchewan listens to kris's wide eyes, quasi stars penetrate the shadow sweeties, fist fights smiling ear to whale, eyes like wet dogs, on durex walking through the inside of a kaleidoscope in a fit of laughter when steve walks up with his clear antenna,

dilated middle finger in the wetness of farewell smiles

in downtown filled bodies.

Legs kick at the ground. Arms flail. Kris is a fish out of water, kicking his way back into a big green lake; his pupils extend over the hazel in his eye, his LED belt buckle emits a blue glow as "PARTY MONSTER" scrolls across the rectangular screen, a comforting numbness fills his pockets, numbness inside-out, his skin dilates, the summer air fills his pores, lilacs blooming on the trees, blooming in the palms of his hands, kissing his olfactories, his neck, behind the ear, jogging towards the little pub down the block, his legs fall onto each other, running on the spot, glare fills the street with a sea of light, ripples and waves close in around him, three figures in the distance stand in the small parking lot of the pub, lamps casts cider across the air, shadows emit presence, bar expands, shadow figures grow, eyes wide, heavy breath, eyes grow at an unequal rate lopsided, *want to fight?, want to?, fight?, WANT TO FIGHT?,* open mouth, jagged teeth, pressured laughter, *WANT TO FIGHT?, something, something,* figures back away, the need buries itself into his hands, his feet, he jumps forward and pushes,   the need exhales, tracers ripple as figures reproach, outlines quiver electric forget this this   this   coarse mesh hair large noses vulgar wrinkled skin thickened bodies expansive hands feet

twisting bulging trolls everywhere holding handlebars
wavering knees bikes on back cement embrace push off
pants push off back dirty grin two men pores breathing

                quavering voice

                   rolling hard

                     rolling

                     pupils

                     burst.

PSILOCYBINZOO

Can anyone ever really know themselves? These people who say shit just to say that they said something—they never expose their insides. Their words are nothing, and their insides are a tree falling in a forest when nobody is around. Comfort is an illness, and I'm only alive if I spend my days in a moderate amount of pain. Or am I only alive if I'm in absolute chaos, and ecstasy?

There are days when I can't tell what's real. There are ghosts of my words that live in her heart, and her spirit follows me. The crescendo of long nights building into a silence so loud that I can't see the ground anymore.

I'm falling down the stairs, and I'm turning into the kraken in my dreams. I'm indoctrinated by the state of our deluded society, love is—love is—love is—love isn't real when we try and press ourselves into the molds of monogamy. I fell in love with chaos again and again, forming hexagons in my heart. I'm trapped in the "I" and I am nothing compared to the beauty of this world.

I arrive at the desolate zoo with Steve thirty minutes after we eat our mushrooms. A statue of Humpty

Dumpty greets us. We find a pond where ducklings swim around and up to the fingertips of children. We, too, extend our hands towards the plump little mounds of yellow fur, our palms full of a quarter's worth of pellets. Sweet puff balls on black webbed feet. The water starts to shimmer. Sun screams through the ripples. The ducklings' little eyes burst into me.

"Let's go to the petting zoo."

I pull Steve's hand away from the little webbed feet towards a gate. I open it to see a goat, but I'm overwhelmed by its hooves.

We go to the nocturnal exhibit but there is nothing to see. I can't stop laughing at that. Blackness and leaves and glass and nothing to see.

Outside, we find a trail that leads us up towards the birds. We find some cages lined up by a fence.

There are little brown owls, and white owls, and, in the last cage—I burst out laughing. A giant bald eagle is sitting in a nest on the ground. How fucking sad is this? I'm bent over, holding my knees as my stomach squeezes in. It's too majestic to be sitting in this little box. What does it do for fun? It must be bored as fuck. I'd be poking out my eyeballs if I was able to spend my life dancing in the sky, then become trapped in a box, and the only window outside is a wall of bars.

Steve and I find a little ice cream stand. The pictures of the different types of popsicles are vibrating with colour. I want to eat the gumball eyeballs of a Sonic the Hedgehog.

We huddle together on a bench as we unwrap Sonic. His face looks distorted, mouth almost below his chin. I giggle and squeeze Steve's knees.

Steve pulls out the bag of shrooms. "Should we take some more?"

We chew down bits of stem as we stare into each other's eyes.

Holding hands, we wander away from our gumball-eyeball feast, and soon find ourselves staring at the elephant.

Elephant to giraffe to grass.

Toy store. Soft toys. Softness in my hands.

Fingers across the back of a turtle. Fingers across the eyes of elephants.

Fuzzy hands.

Twirling fabric.

Laughter.

In a bed, I'm swimming over a blanket with a person who is watching a movie about a fat man dressed in bright rubber clothes. *Who is he?* I poke his face. He is putting little colourful balls in his mouth. I wonder who he is. I poke him. I poke the little balls. I poke his toes. He smiles at me, but his smile is suspicious. Does he know who I am? I can't open my mouth, so I keep pressing my fingers into his skin.

He pulls my hand into his as he laughs and says, "Please, stop."

On the TV, bright red skin-tight suits. Blue glitter tops. Moustached man.

His face is one hundred faces.

I like the grass when it appears in the background. The green is piercing, but in the way a close hug feels on the inside.

I look back at the guy in this bed.

"Steve?"

"Ronnie?"

"I think I forgot who I was for a while there. I forgot who you were."

MISPLACED ENDS

Trees that sing their last song. A song of precious moments before pain, of the last time they knew their names. I'm wondering where the trees go when their trunks are sawed in two. Roots that whimper for the last time. I'm so sorry. Have you ever seen the way two drunk lovers sit on the edge of the river, waiting for the fish to kiss their feet? The river spoke: "I've never been so alone." He said I should stop crying, he said that I should laugh more.

It has been seven days since I bathed myself. I don't know where I've been going this whole time. There are only lights and darks.

And then I'm standing at a bus stop.

"I like your hair."

A younger girl beside me, smiling.

"What?"

She repeats, "I like your hair."

"Oh." I touch my head. "Thanks."

It's short, knotted, and covered in grease. Seven days. I smile back at her before hopping on the next bus.

ECSTASY GHOSTS

Thana had to force me to take a shower. I still can't remember how he broke things off. I was with him, and the next thing I knew I was wandering around, lost inside myself and in the city.

Thana passes me two red pills. She swallows hers with Diet Pepsi.

"Let's walk while these kick in."

The pills taste like they could be made out of the cheap metal rings that leave green stains around my fingers. They slowly move down my throat, further towards my stomach.

The Diet Pepsi barely does anything for the taste.

We throw on our sweaters and shoes before finding ourselves on the wooden stairs that lead us down into the river valley.

Every tree is full and green in the moonlight. We hold hands as our feet take each step down the dimly lit staircase. There isn't enough light and I can feel Thana's grip get tighter when we pass through the darker areas of the path. Our feet move from wood to sidewalk, changing the tone of our journey. The lamp above us goes out.

Thana flinches and mutters, "Fuck, I hate when they do that."

The yellow circles around the streetlights begin to expand; their beams begin to grope at the pavement.

"I think it's kicking in."

"Yeah."

Then, our feet lighten, and the sound of the river pulsates in my ears and I am in love with the world. We walk out on the river docks.

"This is fucking perfect," I say as I start to jump on the docks. "This is everything."

Thana jumps and laughs. She pulls me in and kisses me. Her beauty vibrates through my lips, through my body. The insides of my skin crawl in a bed made out of the softest moss and flower petals. This is where the fairies live.

Love

wonder when i'll see her again

i've been grieving my sobriety

forgot to smudge today

and for the last twenty years

wishing for the smell

of incense and candles

i can feel my heart

everywhere.

Thana pulls her lips away with a warm sigh, and we look out across the river. I nuzzle my head into hers.

Her body jolts back—"Did you see that?"

I look out, but everything is the same.

"The tower over there," she points. "It just fell."

I squint, but there are only dark outlines of trees across the river with a few stars above.

"I don't see any tower. Hey—maybe we should head back, now."

She turns, points to the forest behind us. "Can't you see all the people in the trees?"

I walk into the shadows. "Nothing's here. Let's just go home."

I pull her back up to the main road, and she remains silent except for little gasps as her head twists side to side. Her tense, anxious fingers in my hand drain the euphoria from my mind. The wooden stairs creak beneath our hurried pace.

On the road, drunks cry out from around the convenience store while a dog responds with deep, ferocious barking. Speed from the ecstasy floods my thoughts with clamorous songs of anxiety. Doors slamming people screaming thuds sirens howling coyote the breaking of night air clenched fists in my mind. I try to pull Thana forward to match my faster pace, but her mind is stuck in the empty spaces of the streets.

We arrive at our apartment, and the familiar moldy smell mixed with a fresh scent of curry fills me with relief. I lock the door behind us, try to catch my breath.

The sheets have fallen from the bed again, but I curl into the warmth of our fleece blankets. Thana remains standing on the other side of the room, and I ask her to sit down. Her eyes are on the walls as she says, "Don't you see them?"

I just want this night to end.

"Thana, it's just us here. You're freaking me out."

She finally lets her eyes meet mine, and frowns.

"I'm sorry."

"It's okay—just come sit with me, please."

She takes a few slow steps towards me, edging around nothingness, before she jumps into the bed. Her pupils are massive, like pieces of black onyx. Her lips are perfect, especially when she smiles. I giggle and kiss her forehead. I ask, "Are you okay?"

"Yes, but—it's so strange. I can see people everywhere."

"I don't see anyone," I say. "I don't feel so high at all."

She reaches up to rub at my hairline. I close my eyes.

I don't want her to stop.

She asks, "Should we put on some music, or a movie?"

I flip through my case of CDs until I find an album by I Can Make a Mess Like Nobody's Business. I put it in and press play. When I turn around, Thana leaps out of bed, walks into the corner where she crouches down and extends her hand.

"What are you doing?"

"They're having a party in here! One of them is offering me a drink."

I pull her back to bed. "Please, can you stop this. There's nobody here but us."

Back in bed, I hold her hand and shut my eyes again, letting the music cradle me.

When I open my eyes, I look back at Thana. A guy is sitting behind her, one of my friends from the mall. His arms around her, his chin is resting on her shoulder. They both smile at me. I nearly fall off the bed as I cry out, "What the fuck, Thana."

But, I blink, and he's gone.

when we see things that aren't there

does it mean we are psychotic

or is it because our third eye is

the one which sees most clearly ?

connecting dots in my mind

einstein on methamphetamine

writing on the windows

it was clear as the funnel clouds

that i saw many nights before

SALVIA

Spinning, flipping out, flipping off the people we love. She's crawling in the unsolicited advice of men at bus stations. Smile, they say, and she smiles. Clouds made out of sleepless nights and the way the night opens up the third eye. Forgotten options, legs can't move. She only listens to music made by sad rappers and cocaine addicts. Hid GHB in her water bottle, aching for glow sticks and closed curtains.

Thana passes me the bong and I take a hit. Salvia smoke runs up into my mouth.

I disappear.

Floating in light.

It's blinding and then a bunch of people are flashing past me. It feels like I'm picking a song out of a jukebox. Unfamiliar faces flood out until I see Thana and reach out to grab her, smiling with my eyes shut as I pull her in. She laughs. Then I'm back in our room, on the bed. She asks if I'm okay.

I laugh and say, "I want to do it again!"

PUSH AND BLOW

I arrive at the party with Thana and her new boyfriend, Matty. I clutch my plastic bag with its six-pack of Smirnoff Ice. The house is close to the university, and the air is different here compared to the west end and the east side. Dark wood trim and hardwood floors. The walls are painted in dark blues and greens.

I whisper, "Whose house is this?"

"This guy, Will," Thana says as she pulls off her little white sneakers. "I think his parents gave him and his brother this house last year, when he graduated."

I pull off my slouchy black boots, but all I want to do is leave. All of the girls look so normal here, so pure. Long soft hair, and matching clothing. I feel so dark in my black hair and my deep-blue pleather jacket.

We open our drinks in the kitchen. Names and faces blur in circles. Everyone looks so much older, here. Mature and strange. They laugh about what they did last weekend.

One of the taller guys asks me, "Where are you from?"

"This place in the Northwest Territories—Fort Smith."

"Ah." He takes a swig from his red solo cup as he glances over my body. "Wanna talk somewhere more private?"

He leads me out of the kitchen. Thana raises her eyebrows at me as we pass her, and I shrug my shoulders while grinning back. He takes me downstairs, where the lights are dim. The room is full of people dancing to Snoop Dogg, and he looks back at me as he guides me through, beckons me into a small cement room with a washer and dryer along the wall. Shuts the door behind us. I'm relieved when he doesn't turn the light off.

I take another drink, ask, "So, did you go to school with Matty?"

"No, I went to Scona."

He puts his arm around my waist and pulls me into him. He has to slouch for his lips to meet mine. His face and lips are soft. I press myself into him, but he pulls his face back, looks into my eyes and says, "So, are you going to suck my dick or what?"

I laugh. "Uh, I'm not going to just suck your dick on command."

"What?" he says. "Why else would you follow me down here?"

I take a step back. His face is vacant, except for the slight furrow in his brow. I open the door and say, "Sorry, this is too weird," before I leave the room.

I run up to the kitchen for another drink. I can't find

Thana or her boyfriend, but the beat of a Lil Wayne track rises up from the basement like a flood. I follow it back down, shut my eyes as I try to dance through the cloud of body heat and expensive tracksuits.

Suddenly, hands push hard at my shoulders and I'm falling. My eyes open just before my body slams against the floor. Standing above me is a brown guy with a flashy white hoodie. He smirks as he lifts up his chin. I can feel others looking at me, but everyone continues to dance.

I start to shake. My body feels like it's disintegrating. Tears choke me from the inside. I push myself off the ground and run back upstairs.

Thana is near the door with Matty, and her face drops when she sees the state of mine. She pulls me into the bathroom, tears me off some toilet paper before she asks what happened. I sob into the toilet paper, curl into the floor. I barely get my words out through the tears.

Thana says, "Shit, well—maybe stay upstairs with me. Everyone here's been nice."

"Nobody even tried to help me. Nobody cares if a guy pushes a girl. Nobody cares if a guy is trying to force someone to suck his dick."

She puts her arms around me. "I know—guys are

fucked. But, Matty ordered pizza. Once it gets here, we can just eat and leave, okay?"

I blow my nose into the toilet paper.

>
> *lost hundreds of nights blacked out*
>
> *mountains are the tombstones of earth*
>
> *dipping toes and faces in her wake*
>
> > *call out in both sadness and laughter*
> >
> > *scream into the wind between the trees*
>
> *ancestors' songs sit in the back of my throat*
>
> *what do you want to say now?*
>
> > *there are homes in my eyes for you*
> >
> > > *the time the men carried me away*
> > >
> > > *this happened more than once.*

HIGHWAY OF TEARS

Thana, Matty, and I drive further away from Edmonton and out into the country, past rows of pines and oil rigs that look like giant dipping bird toys.

Dip.

Dip.

Dip.

"I had the weirdest dream last night."

Thana turns down the music, "Yeah?"

"I was with Steve again," I say. "We were standing on a coast. Blue emerald lagoons below. We were trying to fish, but he couldn't catch anything. And I tried to put the bait on the hook, but the bait was a fish the size of my palm. I kept fucking up and tore its fins. The little bait fish was still alive, and I just felt so bad for hurting it. I loved the little fish and I was tearing it apart. I wanted it to have a natural death, so I put the hook away and tried to throw it down into the water. But I missed the water, and it landed on the rocks. I started crying, and I looked out across the water, and I could see the ice melting in the distance in the Arctic."

"Ho-*leh*," Thana says.

"That's some crazy metaphorical shit," Matty says. "I

never remember my dreams."

"I wish I'd stop dreaming about Steve."

Thana says, "Yeah—running into an ex is shitty enough as is. Now you have to do it in your sleep?"

We roll into the acreage, full of cars and people setting up their tents. Matty puts up his tent while we fill bottles with orange juice and vodka. We start to drink as the sun sets. There's a bonfire. Boys lift one another over the keg. Tequila in my flask.

I find myself sitting with a cute boy. Thin and long, brown hair. Looks like he spends his free time playing guitar and writing beautiful songs. I want to hear his songs. It's too dark here, no moon or stars. I want to stay under the light with him while the others crowd the keg and the fire.

Everything disappears.

I'm standing in the middle of a living room, near the TV. I'm mostly naked. A guy's hands are all over me as I sway.

Everything disappears, again.

I wake up on a leather couch. Naked with a blanket over me. A guy with short dirty blonde hair lies on the other couch, across the room, doing something on his phone.

I say, "Hi," but he doesn't look up. I stand up, holding the blanket around me. My clothes are on the floor. I try to pull on my underwear with the blanket wrapped underneath my arms.

I ask him, "Where's my purse?"

"You didn't have it." My stomach turns numb. I need to leave.

The tents. Party. Fire. Tequila flask. The light and the sweet boy. Naked and nothingness.

"Where am I?"

"Sherwood Park."

Still not looking up from his phone, he says, "So, you gonna leave?"

I want to vomit from my tear ducts. I want to scream from the vocal cords in my hands.

"I need to get back to the acreage. Can you drive me?"

"No. You can take a cab, though."

"I don't have my purse, all my money—I don't know how to go."

He pulls out his wallet, passes me a $20 bill.

My body is nothing. I am nothing to him, and there is nothing I can do to change his mind. He calls a cab. I go outside to wait in the heat.

I tell the cab driver where I think I need to go: Range Road 215.

"That's pretty far—I'll need a deposit."

"My bag was stolen last night. I only have this twenty."

He rolls his eyes and I am nothing. "That's not enough. I'll drive you as far as twenty takes you."

Naked and nothing. I want to stitch together the fragments in my mind, but it's like I only exist in the space between them. I'm not anyone anymore. We pass open fields of pale yellow wheat, bright yellow canola. I just need to put my body back where it belongs. I hold my breath as I watch the fare rise to $19.95.

He pulls over on the side of the highway. I get out and watch as he pulls a U-turn, disappears.

The sky is so blue. Small, soft clouds. The sun burns my eyes, heats the pavement so that I sweat from the legs up. I have to keep walking as quickly as possible. I need to put my body back where it belongs.

What if I die here?

Why do I keep doing this to myself?

Why does nobody care? All memory is asphyxiated.

This thirst makes me feel so weak.

he left me crying by the river where i held the grass in my hands depression erupting; sick world sick men sick dicks sick fucks sick cops sick judges sick lawyers sick systems a whole world left me there

alone wondering why a man's lust
                is worth more than a girl's sanity

    it was such a beautiful day by the river
where he left me
       blue sky sitting in the water — it was so perfect

I'm not sure how much time has passed when a familiar car drives by, going in the opposite direction. I hope they don't see me.

The sound of the car turning around sends me into knots of shame. The green Jeep pulls up beside me, and it's one of Thana's friends. He calls out, "Shit, Ronnie, are you okay?"

"Yeah. I don't know. I just need to get back."

"What happened?"

"I don't know."

Someone in the back opens the door, passes me his water bottle. Nobody says a word. I need to put my body back where it belongs. We drive past field after yellow field until we reach the acreage. I thank them for driving me, but my eyes and body still aren't where they should be. I can't look up at them. Naked and nothing until I see Thana running towards me.

HANDEAD

We're driving home some weirdos. There are four of us squeezed into the back of Thana's car. I'm singing along to the music when a hand invades my ass. I tell him to stop, but he won't take his hand away, going deeper in between my cheeks. I start to sob. I punch and shake him off of me, but I can't stop crying. Thana pulls into a parking lot, kicks him out of the car and tells him to fuck off. We start to drive away, but the ass-grabbing dude starts yelling at us—and instead of driving away, Thana turns the car back towards him.

everything looks the same,

The ass-grabbing dude waves his arms, shouts, walks towards the car until Thana speeds right into him.

the tower, the dial tone

THUNK. THUNK.

six hands of depression erupting

He rolls over the hood and over the windshield.

sun burns my eyes

as i say, "isn't this pretty?"

Two more THUNKs and he's lying on the ground behind us.

We pull out of the parking lot. The shadow of his body fades into the night.

i just need to become a full-time shadow

I am soaring, euphoric.

kicks him out

tells him to go dance with the new moon

His body rolling over the windshield replays in my mind, again and again.

Each time with a new face.

AFTERWORD

Mahsi cho for reading.

I want to leave you with a little story.

I was an extremely imaginative and sensitive child. I had no problem with being alone, because in my mind, I could create anything. One day, early in kindergarten before I had any friends, I was playing in the trees alone at recess. It was a beautiful day. Blue skies and green everywhere. I was prancing around, pretending I was hanging out with some fairies, when my wiggling tooth popped out of my mouth. It fell on the ground, and since I had a fear of blood, I started to cry. But I still needed to bring this tooth home to give it to the tooth fairy. So, I bent down to pick up the tooth, and in that moment, I heard a plop and my hair suddenly felt all warm and wet. A bird had took a shit on my head. At this point, I went from crying to really crying. I ran to the school, holding my bloody tooth out in one hand and my shit-covered hair in the other. When I told my aunty Delphine this story, she said it means I'm lucky.

MAHSI CHO

To my editor A. Light Zachary, Ashley Obscura, CAConrad, Anne Boyer, and everyone at Metatron; I am so grateful for all your love and support. I've been crying tears of joy ever since I made it onto the shortlist. And I've been crying more and more with each step in this journey towards the publication of this book. Thank you.

To my nieces Madeline and Sarah, and my nephew Ryley for being the coolest (Aunty loves you all so much!). To all my relatives from Fort Smith and Ottawa, I feel so fortunate for all your love and for each time I'm able to visit with you. Most of all to Mom and Dad, and to my sisters Hailea, Lorrie, and Melissa. I love you all to the moon and back. You all inspire me to be better every day. I wouldn't have made it into and through university without all of your unconditional love and support. Mahsi cho.

To all my friends and teachers who brought me back from flunking out of high school, and again when I tried upgrading my high school courses, and again when I entered university. Thank you for believing in me even though I have ADHD, am usually too spaced out to participate, and am just terribly chronically late.

You are all angels. Special thanks to Joel Katelnikoff for inspiring me to take risks in my writing, and pushing me to give it my all. 2014 was one of the most difficult years in my life, but being in your class really helped transform my grief into freedom.

To my master's thesis supervisor Christine Stewart for creating spaces for Indigenous students to exist and thrive in the university. You are just a hero in all that you do for all your students. Thank you to everyone else that was part of my thesis defence at the University of Alberta. Tom Wharton, Trudy Cardinal, and Keavy Martin: thank you for crying and laughing with me and making that day extra special.

Special thanks to everyone in the Writing Revolution in Place creative research collective, who have kept me connected to Edmonton even after moving away. Les Danyluk, Roberta Kreuger, Zeny Marte, James McDonald, Keighlagh Donovan, Rob Keith, Ximena Flores Ouiedo, and Mackenzie Ground. I love you I love you I love you.

I feel so fortunate to have so many loved ones, so many dear friends over the years, from Edmonton to Calgary, and all the friends I've made through the Banff Centre. Thank you for putting up with me in my bad days and thank you for making my good days so much brighter. You all have taught me so much and have made my heart so full.

So much gratitude to the music scene in Edmonton. Going to shows like Lazersnake, Feast or Famine, The Joe, and Cadence Weapon always kept me so inspired during my adolescent years.

I also need to thank the visual artist Hernan Bas for his beautiful work. I do not know where I would be if I hadn't found a small print of his piece The Swan Prince in one of my art classes. I fell in love.

KAITLYN PURCELL is an artist, poet, storyteller, and scholar. She is a proud member of Smith's Landing First Nation, and the Writing Revolution in Place creative research collective. She is a PhD student at the University of Calgary studying Indigenous Literatures, Creative Writing, and Community-Based Learning. Her work is inspired by her experiences as a troubled adolescent in Edmonton, detached from her Dene roots. She has received numerous awards for her creative work, such as the Metatron Prize for Rising Authors (2018) and the Alberta Foundation for the Arts Young Artist Prize (2017). *ʔbédayine* was nominated for an Indigenous Voices Award for Published Prose in English (2020). *ʔbédayine* is her first book.